BOYZ RULE!

Tennis Ace

Felice Arena and Phil Kettle

illustrated by
Susy Boyer

First published 2003 by
MACMILLAN EDUCATION AUSTRALIA PTY LTD
627 Chapel Street, South Yarra, Australia 3141

This edition first published in the United States of America
in 2004 by MONDO Publishing.

For information contact:
MONDO Publishing
980 Avenue of the Americas
New York, NY 10018

Visit our web site at http://www.mondopub.com

04 05 06 07 08 09   9 8 7 6 5 4 3 2 1

ISBN 1-59336-360-5 (PB)

Library of Congress Cataloging-in-Publication Data

Arena, Felice, 1968-
    Tennis ace / Felice Arena and Phil Kettle ; illustrated by Susy Boyer.
    p. cm. -- (Boyz rule!)
    Summary: Dreaming of being tennis professionals, Jamal and Joey head to
    the park to practice. Includes simple tennis facts and questions to test the
    reader's comprehension.
    ISBN: 1-59336-360-5 (pbk.)
    [1. Tennis--Fiction.] I. Kettle, Phil, 1955- II. Boyer, Susy, ill. III. Title.

PZ7.A6825Te 2004
[E]--dc22

                                                          2004047053

Project Management by Limelight Press Pty Ltd
Cover and text design by Lore Foye
Illustrations by Susy Boyer

Printed in Hong Kong

Contents

Jamal   *Joey*

CHAPTER 1

Tennis Tactics

The U.S. Open tennis tournament is played once a year. To win the title of best player takes a lot of really hard training. So Jamal and Joey have been training really hard! Every afternoon after school they go to the park and practice their tennis. They want to make sure that they are ready to play in this year's U.S. Open.

Jamal arrives at Joey's place,
ready to go to the park.

Jamal "Are you ready to go?"
Joey "I have to have something to
    eat, then I'll be ready."

Jamal "You're always eating."

Joey "That's because I'm always hungry."

Jamal "Maybe you have a big tapeworm living in your stomach."

Joey "No, I don't. I'm just growing fast."

Jamal "Maybe, but if you keep eating so much, you might end up growing out, not up."

Joey "Well, I've finished eating now, so are you ready to go?"

Jamal "I've been ready since I got here."

Joey collects his tennis racquet and together the boys walk to the park.

CHAPTER 2

The Tennis Court

In the middle of the park is a
basketball court. A large brick wall
runs down the side of the court. The
wall has a line painted across it, the
same height as a tennis net.

Jamal "So, are we going to play singles or doubles?"

Joey "Well, I wanna be Andy Roddick—he always wins."

Jamal "Okay. I'll be James Blake—*he's cool!*"

Joey "Well, if that's who you're going to be, then we should play doubles."

Jamal "Why?"

Joey "Because he never wins. He comes in second every time he plays me."

Jamal "If he played *you* all the time he'd *always* win."

Joey "Nah, I'm Andy Roddick so he'd never win against me."

Jamal reaches into his pocket and pulls out a piece of rag.

Joey "What are ya gonna do with that?"

Jamal "Good players always wear a headband."

Joey "Yeah, but great players like
Andy wear their hat backwards."

Joey turns his hat around, like
Andy. Jamal ties on his headband,
then tightens it a bit.

Jamal holds his tennis racquet like a guitar.

Jamal "You know the best thing about having a tennis racquet?"

Joey "You can play tennis with it."

Jamal "Yeah, duh! But when you're not playing tennis, you can use the racquet as a guitar."

Joey "Well, after losing against me, you'll wanna start playing a guitar."

Jamal "Let's start playing and see who's really the loser."

CHAPTER 3

Warm-up

Jamal and Joey start hitting the ball against the brick wall. Jamal hits first. The ball bounces back and Joey makes the next hit.

Joey "Are we playing singles or doubles?"

Jamal "I think we should play doubles."

Joey "Cool. Let's play then."

Andy and James are best buds and they really like playing together.

Jamal "So who are we going to play against?"

Joey "Australia—we always like playing against them."

Jamal "Yeah, and we always beat 'em."

Joey "So what are their players' names?"

Jamal "Why don't we just call them 'Silver?'"

Joey "Why Silver?"

Jamal "Well, that's what you get when you come second."

Jamal hits the ball hard into the brick wall. This time the ball flies back and Joey belts it. The warm-up is complete and the match can begin.

CHAPTER 4

Let the Match Begin

Jamal decides that he'll be the
on-court announcer and that it's
time to introduce the players.

Jamal *"Ladies and gentlemen, today's game on center court is between two great U.S. players, James Blake and Andy Roddick. They are playing against Australia. The Australian players are not up to the standard set by the U.S. players. Their names are Cement Silver and Concrete Silver. They have no hope of winning. The best they can expect to come in is second."*

Jamal "So who's going to serve first?"

Joey "I will. I've got the best serve."

Jamal "Your serve's not better than mine."

Joey "Well, let's say that we both have the best serves in the world."

Jamal "Blake serves the ball. Cement returns the ball. Roddick belts the ball back at Concrete. The ball hits the edge of Concrete's racquet and goes out of bounds."

Joey gives Jamal a high five.

Joey "Great serve, James!"

Jamal "And a great return, Andy!"

Joey "Yeah, we're the best team in the world. Nobody can beat us."

Jamal "Look how quiet Cement and Concrete are. They know we're awesome and are too scared to speak."

Joey "If we keep playing like this they'll never win a point."

Jamal "It could be the first time in history that two great players have never lost a point in a game of tennis."

Jamal serves again.

Joey *"Another great forehand by Roddick."*

Jamal "And that was another great backhand by me."

Joey *"Roddick runs really fast across the court. He's so fast and, yes, he makes another great shot!"*

Jamal "Yes, yours was great, but not as good as the one I'm about to make."

Joey "Well this time I'm going to hit a two-handed, backhand cross-court power shot. The Aussies will never hit this back."
"The Australian pair, Cement and Concrete, still haven't said a word, but they keep getting the ball back into play."

Jamal "The harder we hit the ball at them, the harder they hit it back at us."

Joey "I've got just the shot that'll beat 'em."

Jamal "So what's that?"

Joey "Watch this!"

Joey runs toward the ball and hits it high in the air.

Jamal "What sort of shot is that?"

Joey "It's a lob shot. They'll never be able to get that back."

Jamal "That shot's really cool. We've found their weakness."

Joey "The Aussie players won't be able to get to the ball to return it."

CHAPTER 5

We Are the Champions

Jamal and Joey are beating the team from Australia. They are only one point away from winning the U.S. Open.

Jamal "We only need one more point to win."

Joey "We're the best team in the world."

Jamal "I hit the ball straight down the center of the court."

Joey "But they hit it back. It's up to me. I'll try the lob shot."

The ball floats over the top of the brick wall. The boys throw their racquets up in the air.

Joey "We won! We're the champions!"

Jamal "That was easy. Cement and Concrete might be good in Australia, but they aren't very good when they play us."

Joey "I bet we could beat anyone in the world."

Jamal "Yeah, I bet we're the best in the universe."

Joey "Hey, see that dog running across the park?"

Jamal "Yeah."

Joey "He's got our tennis ball in his mouth."

Jamal "We'd better chase after him
to get the ball back."

Joey "I can run faster than you."

Jamal "Here we go again!"

Jamal

Tennis Lingo

Joey

ace When you serve the ball and the player you have served the ball to cannot hit it back.

doubles When two players play together as a team against two other players.

lob When you hit the ball really high into the air.

net This runs across the center of the court. You have to hit the ball over the net.

singles When one tennis player plays against another tennis player.

Tennis Musts

☞ Make sure that the brick wall you are playing against is made of smooth bricks.

☞ If you want to be just like Andy Roddick, make sure you wear your cap backwards.

☞ If you want to be like Andre Agassi, wear really baggy shorts and shave your head.

☞ Learn to hit forehand shots as well as backhand shots.

☞ Remember that the harder you hit the ball against the brick wall, the faster the ball will come back at you.

☞ Don't throw your racquet when you make a bad shot.

☞ Try to wear really cool-looking clothes.

☞ When you are playing, pretend that you are at the U.S. Open and playing on center court.

☞ If you start to get bored, turn the racquet around and pretend that you are playing a guitar.

BOYZ RULE!

Tennis Instant Info

Pete Sampras has won Wimbledon the most times—seven.

Boris Becker is the youngest player to win the Wimbledon men's singles title. He was 17 years old.

The longest rally (not in a tournament) is one that lasted 17,062 strokes. The rally lasted for 9 hours and 6 minutes.

You serve a fault if you serve the ball outside the service lines marked on the court.

A deuce is when the scores in a game are even at three points each.

A ball boy can also be a girl and is the person who collects the balls on the court between points.

In tennis the word "love" means zero. It's used to show that a person hasn't scored a point.

37

BOYZ RULE!

Think Tank

1 Which players do Jamal and Joey pretend to be?

2 What happens to the tennis ball at the end of their game?

3 In which city is the U.S. Open held?

4 What is an *ace* in tennis?

5 What is the total number of players in a doubles game of tennis?

6 When the umpire calls "let," what has happened?

7 What do you think is more important to being a great tennis player: talent or lots of practice? Why?

8 Is tennis one of your favorite sports to play? Why? Do you like playing or watching tennis better? Why?

Answers

8 Answers will vary.

7 Answers will vary.

6 "Let" means that the ball you serve touches the top of the net before falling into the serving court.

5 There is a total of four players in a game of doubles.

4 An *ace* is when the ball is served so that the player receiving it cannot hit it back.

3 The U.S. Open is held in New York City.

2 A dog runs away with their tennis ball in its mouth.

1 Jamal pretends to be James Blake, and Joey pretends to be Andy Roddick.

How did you score?

- If you got most of the answers correct, then you might be ready to be a professional tennis player.

- If you got more than half of the answers correct, you need a little more coaching.

- If you got less than half of the answers correct, then keep practicing against the brick wall.

Felice →   ← Phil

Hi Guys!

We have lots of fun reading and want you to, too. We both believe that being a good reader is really important and so cool.

Try out our suggestions to help you have fun as you read.

At school, why don't you use "Tennis Ace" as a play and you and your friends can be the actors. Set the scene for your play. Maybe you can take your tennis racquet to school or maybe you can just use your imagination to pretend that you are on center court at the U.S. Open.

So...have you decided who is going to be Jamal and who is going to be Joey? Now, with your friends, read and act out our story in front of the class.

We have a lot of fun when we go to schools and read our stories. After we finish, the kids all clap really loudly. When you've finished your play your classmates will do the same. Just remember to look out the window—there might be a talent scout from a television station watching you!

Reading at home is really important and a lot of fun as well.

Take our books home and get someone in your family to read them with you. Maybe they can take on a part in the story.

Remember, reading is a whole lot of fun.

So, as the frog in the local pond would say, Read-it!

And remember, Boyz Rule!

When We Were Kids

Felice

Phil

Felice "What kind of juice did you think they were talking about in tennis when you were a kid? Apple? Orange?"

Phil "It's *deuce*, not *juice*, you goof!"

Felice "Yeah, I know. I was just joking."

Phil "Well, I'm thirsty. I think I might go and have a glass of deuce."

Felice "Don't you mean *juice*?"

Phil "Yeah, orange deuce."

Felice "You're weird! How did you ever play tennis when you were a kid if you don't know the difference between *deuce* and *juice*?"

Phil "That's just it—I didn't!"

BOYZ RULE!

What a Laugh!

Q Which tennis player can jump higher than the net?

A All of them— a tennis net can't jump.